I WAS ALL ALONE—

Lisa and I ran for the escalator, trying to escape from the shopping mall. The ride up to the second level seemed to take forever. I could swear the escalator slowed to half speed as soon as we stepped on. When I got off at the top, I turned to tell Lisa to hurry.

I couldn't believe it. She wasn't there!

"Lisa!" I shrieked, jumping up and down. "Lisa, where are you?"

I looked down the escalator as it continued its slow rise to the second floor.

Lisa wasn't there. She was gone.

Lisa had vanished.

I was all alone—trapped in the mall.

Read these other BONE CHILLERS from
HarperPaperbacks

BONE CHILLERS

BEWARE THE SHOPPING MALL

BETSY HAYNES

HarperPaperbacks

A Division of HarperCollins*Publishers*

HarperPaperbacks *A Division of* HarperCollins*Publishers*
10 East 53rd Street, New York, N.Y. 10022

Copyright © 1994 by Betsy Haynes and
Daniel Weiss Associates, Inc.

Cover art copyright © 1994 Daniel Weiss Associates, Inc.

All rights reserved. No part of this book may be used or reproduced in any manner whatsoever without written permission of the publisher, except in the case of brief quotations embodied in critical articles and reviews. For information address Daniel Weiss Associates, Inc., 33 West 17th Street, New York, New York 10011.

Produced by Daniel Weiss Associates, Inc., 33 West 17th Street, New York, New York 10011.

First printing: February, 1994

Printed in the United States of America

HarperPaperbacks and colophon are trademarks of HarperCollins*Publishers*

10 9 8 7 6 5

For Frankenstein, The Wolf Man, The Mummy, Dracula, and all the rest of my spooky friends

BEWARE THE
SHOPPING MALL

Chapter

"**W**onderland Mall Opens Today!" I shouted happily.

I read the giant billboard aloud as Mom drove past it and followed the long stream of traffic into the main parking area for the new shopping mall.

"This is where Mournful Swamp used to be when I was your age." Mom looked over at me and chuckled. "It was a da-a-ark and scary place, filled with quicksand and deep ravines and monsters," she said, trying to sound spooky. "I'll never forget when three teenagers disappeared in the swamp. It was back when I was in high school. Everybody assumed they walked into quicksand and were sucked under, but nobody really knows what happened to them. Remember that story?"

I nodded. Who cared about that stuff? It was ancient history. Wonderland Mall was the most exciting thing that had happened to the town of Meadowdale in a long, long time. It wouldn't have mattered to me if it had been built on top of a graveyard.

"For years people were too frightened to come near this place," Mom went on. "Everybody said it was haunted. Can you believe they'd actually build a mall out here? Oooh, it gives me the creeps."

I grinned at her and shrugged. "That's progress, I guess. Wow! Would you check that out!"

The new mall had just come into sight. It was humongous, with multicolored banners fluttering in the breeze. Moving spotlights danced over it, creating a spectacular light show. The main part of the mall was three stories high. I had read in the paper that it had six movie screens, a video arcade, a food court, an ice-skating rink, and dozens of stores. I could hardly wait to see for myself.

I took a deep breath and stared up at the colossal mall. I was imagining shopping *big time* with my friends, pigging out at the food court, and maybe even catching a movie.

"Mom, can't we go a little faster?" I pleaded. "I'm already late!"

Mom snorted in exasperation and gestured at

the slow-moving traffic ahead of us. "Only if this car sprouts wings and flies. You know this is the big opening day. The whole town is here."

I sighed and slumped against the passenger door. I was supposed to meet some friends by the main entrance to the mall at eight A.M. And it was already eight fifteen. We had to be among the first one hundred shoppers in the front door when the mall opened at nine o'clock to get a chance at a lottery for a free trip to Hawaii. I was dying to go to Hawaii.

Traffic was moving at a crawl as long lines of cars snaked up and down the parking-lot rows, searching for empty spaces. Suddenly I had an idea.

"Why don't you just let me out here?" I blurted. "I can make better time on foot. Thanks, Mom. I'll call you when I'm ready to come home."

I jumped out of the barely moving car before Mom could argue. Then I tossed her a quick smile and a wave over my shoulder and zigzagged through the traffic toward the main entrance to Wonderland Mall. I groaned when I saw the size of the crowd that was already forming at the door.

"Over here! Over here!"

I looked toward the shouts and saw Lisa, Shannon, and Eric at the edge of the crowd. They were waving wildly. "Robin Fagin, where have you been?" Lisa demanded, flipping a strand of dark curly hair over one shoulder. Lisa Karl was really cute, and the first thing everyone noticed about her was her beautiful thick hair and her big smile. "Look at all the people who are already ahead of us."

"I got here as fast as I could," I grumbled. "Besides, I don't see Jamie."

"She isn't here yet," said Eric, gazing up the long driveway leading from the highway to the entrance of the mall. Even though Eric Sandifer was part of our group of friends, being around him made me a little jittery sometimes. I had a secret crush on Eric, and I would die if anyone ever found out. He was tall and slim and athletic, and he had an incredible dimple in his chin when he smiled.

"She said she was coming on the bus," said Shannon Markoff, pushing her wire-frame glasses up on her nose. "Since the mall is the last stop on the bus line, and since it's opening day, I bet it was so crowded she couldn't get on. She probably had to wait for a later bus."

I looked through the crowd again. Jamie England's short-cut white-blond hair and huge blue eyes were hard to miss, even in a crowd like this. But I didn't see her anywhere.

"Come on, guys, we can't wait forever," urged Shannon. She pushed her glasses up on her nose again and looked around anxiously. The crowd had grown even bigger while we stood there talking.

"Video Showcase is giving away T-shirts. I'm going to kill Jamie if I don't get one!" said Shannon. "Just look at how many people are ahead of us."

The instant she got the words out, a large lady wearing a purple raincoat rushed past us, heading for the crowded entrance and shoving Shannon aside as she went by.

"Geez!" said Shannon, frowning after the lady. "This place is a zoo. We'll never get inside in time to get in on the drawing for the trip to Hawaii."

"Hey, everybody! Look over there," said Eric. He was pointing to a side entrance where a sign on the door said Employees Only. "Maybe we could go in there and sneak into the main part of the mall ahead of the crowd."

"Get serious," said Lisa. She tossed her curly head impatiently. "We're not employees."

"Besides, it's probably locked," I said dejectedly.

"There's one way to find out," said Shannon. She marched straight to the door and gave it a tug.

It swung open.

We looked at each other, hesitating.

5

"We could get into big trouble if anybody caught us," Lisa warned.

"Get real, Lisa," Shannon said with a grin. "Who's going to catch us?"

Then she stepped inside.

Chapter

"Maybe we should have waited for Jamie. She'll never find us now," I said as soon as the door clanged shut behind us. We were in a long empty corridor. My voice sounded unusually loud as it echoed off the walls.

"Shhh," cautioned Lisa. She raised a finger to her lips and frowned at me.

I frowned back at her. "We really aren't supposed to be here, you know. We could get in big trouble."

"Come on, guys," Shannon said. "Don't any of you wimp out. Let's see if we can find the main part of the mall." She pushed her glasses up on her nose and stared down the long silent hallway.

"Yeah," said Eric, "there's nothing to worry about. We're all alone down here."

7

I followed the others past empty offices on either side of the hall. The lights were off in all the offices.

I sighed with relief. "I guess it's too early in the morning for anyone to be at work yet."

Eric nodded and gave me a sort of half smile that made his dimple appear really fast and then disappear again. "So far, so good."

"Right," I said, staring at his chin.

"Will you two be quiet?" Lisa cautioned again. She frowned over her shoulder at Eric and me.

"Don't be so bossy," I grumbled under my breath. Then I stuck my tongue out at the back of her head.

We crept through the corridors, rounding first one corner and then another, looking for the way into the main part of the mall. We turned into a hallway where all the doors were closed, and every few seconds I threw an anxious glance over my shoulder in case someone came up behind us.

Just as we turned another corner, Shannon stopped dead in her tracks. It caused a chain-reaction collision. Lisa barreled into Shannon. Eric barreled into Lisa. And I barreled into Eric.

Shannon's eyes opened wide, and she pointed to a man coming toward us. He was tall and bulky, with a deeply tanned face and a full head of white hair. He was wearing a dark business suit, and he was busily reading some papers as he hurried along. And he looked mean—real mean.

"Quick, find some place to hide before he sees us!" Shannon said in a loud whisper.

I started backpedaling as fast as I could. I searched frantically for an empty room to duck into. But the doors along the corridor were all locked!

The man still hadn't seen us, but any minute he could finish reading his papers and look up. What if he caught us? What if he called the security guards? What if he had us arrested for trespassing?

In desperation I tried one door after another until one finally opened. "In here!" I called.

The room was pitch-black and stuffy, but at first I was too relieved to care. My legs were rubbery, and my hands were shaking. As I leaned against the door to catch my breath, I could hear my pulse pounding in my ears.

"I wonder where we are." Eric's voice came from somewhere in the darkness.

"I don't know, but I don't like it," Lisa squeaked from another direction.

"Hey, everybody," said Shannon. Her usually chirpy voice was deadly serious. "I hate to tell you this, but I think we have company."

My eyes were beginning to adjust to the darkness. I blinked and looked around. I could make out the forms of my friends now as the blackness softened into deep gray. Lisa and Eric were stand-

9

ing to my left, and Shannon was just behind them. But who was that fourth person in the middle of the room? And the fifth and sixth and seventh near the other wall?

I stuffed a fist into my mouth to stifle a cry. I could see pretty clearly now. The room was the size of a classroom. And it was filled with people. Dozens of them.

Silent, motionless people. Some adults. Some children. Some sitting. Some standing.

And every one of them was staring straight at me.

Chapter

Suddenly Shannon burst out laughing.

"They're only mannequins," she cried. "A whole roomful of dummies."

I giggled nervously and looked at the figures again. Shannon was right. They were just a bunch of plastic dummies. Some of them had arms missing. Or legs. One female mannequin near me didn't have a head!

"I think we stumbled into a storage room," I said in a breathy whisper. "This place is too weird. Let's get out of here."

"Be careful," Lisa said as we moved toward the door that would take us back into the corridor. "That man could still be out there."

"Hey, wait a minute," said Shannon. "There's another door over here. Let's see where it goes. Maybe it's the one we've been looking for. The one to the main floor of the mall."

Shannon was already heading for the second door. Eric followed. And Lisa skittered after them like a frightened mouse.

I hesitated, pinned to the spot where I was standing by the sightless eyes of the mannequins. I couldn't shake the feeling that they were really watching me. Following my every move.

"Come on, slowpoke," called Shannon. She reached for the door and turned the knob.

I started toward my friends, holding my breath as I tiptoed past the ghostly figures. A large cardboard box sat directly in my path. As I walked around it, I stiffened and stopped cold. A jumble of mannequin heads were in the box. A jumble of heads that were all looking up at me.

"Eeek!" I shrieked and jumped back.

"What's the matter?" Eric asked.

I took a deep breath to slow the pounding of my heart. No matter which way each head was facing in the box, its eyes seemed to be turned on me.

"Oh, nothing," I said as casually as I could. "Just heads. Mannequin heads."

If I told my friends what I'd seen, they'd think I was totally freaking out.

I caught up with them just as they disappeared through the door, and clanked behind them down a flight of metal stairs. A soft light burned below.

12

"I don't think this is where we want to be," said Eric as we clustered at the bottom of the stairs outside still another door. He looked less confident than he had before.

"Cluck, cluck, cluck," taunted Shannon. "You guys are such chickens. We should at least find out where we are."

Before anyone could protest, she opened the door just enough to slip through, and disappeared. I felt a blast of cold air as the door slammed shut behind her.

"I think we should get out of here," Lisa said loudly. "It's really creepy down here. We shouldn't have come down those stairs in the first place."

"I agree," said Eric. "Let's split."

"But we can't leave Shannon," I protested.

We stood there, glancing back and forth at each other.

"I wonder why she hasn't come back," Eric said after a while. "I mean, since we didn't come after her, you'd think . . ." His voice trailed off.

"Do you think she's okay?" Lisa murmured.

"I don't know," I said, "but we've got to find out."

I took a deep breath and opened the door. Peering into a shadowy room, I sucked in my breath and shrank back.

"Oh, no!" I shrieked.

13

"What is it?" Eric and Lisa demanded in unison.

All I could do was step aside and point.

Shannon's body was sprawled facedown on the cold concrete floor.

Chapter

S hannon wasn't moving, and it didn't look as if she was breathing either.

The three of us moved slowly toward her and crouched around her still figure.

"Shannon, can you hear me?" I whispered, terrified. I gently nudged Shannon's shoulder. "Shannon, answer me! Are you okay?"

"Couldn't be better," Shannon cried, rolling over and cracking up. "I wish you guys could see your faces right now. What a bunch of chickens."

Eric groaned in exasperation.

Lisa rolled her eyes toward the ceiling.

"Very funny," I said. Sometimes Shannon could be a real jerk.

Shannon jumped to her feet. "Come on, let's get going," she called out. "It's almost opening

15

time. We're going to miss the drawing for the free trip to Hawaii."

"Wait a minute," I said, looking around.

I had just become aware of the dimly lit room we were in. Crouched in the shadows were monstrous machines, pulsing and humming and groaning so hard that the floor vibrated beneath our feet. Over our heads pipes stuck out of the machines and snaked across the ceiling, where they disappeared into the walls.

"We must be in the basement," said Lisa. "These are probably the air-conditioning units for the whole mall."

I knelt on one knee and examined the floor. My eerie feeling was back. "Remember that article in the newspaper a couple of weeks ago about how a crack opened up down here in the basement floor?" I asked.

"I saw that," said Lisa. "The paper said it was right over the spot where the ravine used to be when this was Mournful Swamp."

"Yeah," said Shannon. "They were afraid the mall wouldn't be able to open on time."

"But they cemented it up, and everything was okay," Eric said. "It's funny when you think about it, though. So many creepy things happened while this mall was being built. Remember the dump truck that poured a load of rocks on one of the workmen and killed him?"

"Yeah," I said. That story was especially weird because nobody was at the controls of the truck. It seemed to have been driving itself. The police investigated, and couldn't find anything. So they wound up calling it an accident.

"And a lot of things disappeared mysteriously," said Lisa. "Big pieces of machinery and stuff like that."

"And what about the guy who fell into that vat of wet cement?" Shannon asked.

"I heard they fished around for a long time but couldn't find his body. A lot of people thought the construction sight was jinxed," I said. Then I added hurriedly, "Come on, let's go. I don't like it down here."

I got slowly to my feet. The cemented crack looked like a giant scar. It ran across the floor exactly where Shannon had been lying. I suddenly wondered what would happen if the crack opened up and sucked me under the mall. The thought made me shiver, so I turned quickly and raced after the others.

Just then lights started blinking on one of the giant machines, and the sound it was making changed.

Ay-in. Ay-in. Ay-in.

I stopped, but the others hadn't seemed to notice. I glanced at the machine. The lights had stopped blinking, but the sound was becoming louder and more distinct.

AY-IN. AY-IN. AY-IN.

I frowned. Why didn't anyone else hear it?

AY-IN! AY-IN! AY-IN!

I called out to my friends to listen, but they had already gone through the door. Suddenly it changed again. FA-GIN. FA-GIN. FA-GIN.

Fagin? That was my name! My last name! But a machine couldn't say somebody's name, I reasoned, trying to stay calm.

I reached the door in one gigantic step and bolted out of the room.

Chapter

5

A few minutes later we finally found the main entrance to the mall. The spooky events in the basement seemed so unreal that I didn't mention them to the others. I didn't want them to think I was going psycho or something.

"Wow! Would you look at this!" Shannon cried as we entered the mammoth center court. I watched her spread her arms wide and circle slowly, as I tried to take it all in.

A teenage rock band blasted music from a stage at one end of the center court. At the other end, a jungle of plants and trees surrounded a miniature waterfall. Beside the waterfall shoppers were sitting on benches watching giant goldfish swim lazily in a pond. Everywhere bright helium-filled balloons leaped upward. People bustled in and out of stores. The faint smell of popcorn and hamburgers hung in the air.

"I don't believe it," whispered Lisa. "It's paradise."

"It's *awesome*," I added, spinning around. "I don't know which way to look first."

A giddy sense of carnival magic was everywhere. Smiling people looked down from the railings on the second and third floors. And escalators jammed with laughing shoppers moved slowly up and down. Above it all, sunshine poured through the skylighted roof and settled on everyone like fairy dust.

"I'm starved. I want to find the food court," said Lisa, bouncing impatiently on her toes. "I think it's over there."

"Hey, there's the arcade over there," Eric said, pointing in the opposite direction. "Anybody want to play some video games?"

I made a face. "Food and video games? Are you guys kidding?" I asked. "I came here for one reason, and one reason only: to *shop.*"

"Me, too," said Shannon. "Have you ever seen so many stores in your life? It's unbelievable."

"Welcome to Wonderland Mall!"

A pretty blond girl who didn't look much older than my friends and me was walking toward us, smiling. Her golden hair was long and silky, and she had dazzling blue eyes. She was dressed in a miniskirt and a knockout sweater.

"I know you're going to love the new mall," she said in a perky voice, "and to help you find your way around, here's a map of all the shops and attractions."

She handed each of us a map and mentioned several opening-day sales. Then, turning to leave, she added with a cheery smile, "Have a nice day."

"Gosh, did you check her out?" exclaimed Shannon as the girl moved to another group of shoppers nearby.

Eric nodded and stared after her as if he were in a trance.

"Looks to die for," Lisa murmured, shaking her head.

"Tell me about it," I added, sighing. "She's almost too perfect to be real."

Maps in hand, we headed off to check out the opening-day sales in some of the stores.

"Since it's already nine fifteen, it's too late to get into the lottery for the free trip to Hawaii. Why don't we find Video Showcase and see if they still have any T-shirts to give away?" Shannon suggested. She stopped in the middle of the crowd, almost causing a traffic jam. Pushing her glasses up on her nose, she studied her map. "It's right here," she said, stabbing the map with a finger. "Up on the second level."

Wonderland Mall was getting more crowded by

21

the moment, and we had to stand in line to get on the escalator. It was packed, and we got separated immediately. I ended up riding up to the second floor with my face practically jammed into the back of a tall thin woman with bushy white hair.

"Now, where is this Video Showcase?" I asked Shannon when we had all gotten off the escalator.

"This way," said Shannon. She plunged into the crowd.

I took off after her, but the crowd was so thick that I lost sight both of Shannon and the others immediately.

I wasn't sure where I was going, so I made my way to the balcony railing, stopping in frustration to consult my map. Video Showcase was only a few stores away.

When I reached the video store, the others were already there, waiting outside.

"What happened to you, slowpoke?" asked Shannon, grinning.

"Nothing," I retorted. Then I dashed for the door and entered the store ahead of the others. The instant I got inside, I stopped. My mouth dropped open in surprise.

"Welcome to Video Showcase!"

A blond teenage girl was greeting us at the door. Her golden hair was long and silky. And she had dazzling blue eyes. And she was dressed in a miniskirt and a great-looking sweater.

She was the same girl who had handed us the maps downstairs in the center court a few minutes before. But that was impossible.

How could she be in two places at once?

Chapter

"How did you get up here so quickly?" I asked the blonde.

"Yeah, we just saw you downstairs," said Shannon.

The blonde laughed. "That must have been someone else," she said. "I've been here in Video Showcase ever since the mall opened. This is where I work."

"Oh, come on," scoffed Lisa. "We saw you downstairs. You were handing out maps of the mall."

"It wasn't me," the blond girl said. "Honest."

"Then you've got a twin," said Eric.

"Look, guys." She was starting to sound irritated. "I didn't hand out maps downstairs. I work here in the Video Showcase, and I've been here since nine o'clock. And I don't have a twin. Okay?"

Her face clouded for a second, and then her smile returned. She reached into a cardboard box and pulled out a handful of T-shirts. "Here. Have a free shirt."

We each took a shirt, and then we browsed among the videos and CD's for a couple of minutes before leaving the store.

"That was really weird," said Eric when we were outside. "I could have sworn that she was the same girl we saw downstairs."

I had been thinking about her the whole time we were in the video store. "I bet they really are twins," I said. "It's probably some kind of advertising gimmick that the mall people thought up. Maybe they hired lots of twins and they're going to have a contest to see how many sets people can find."

"Yeah, right, sure, Robin," Shannon said, giving me an oddball look. "Maybe they're going to let us have all the free clothes we want, too."

"It was only an idea," I responded defensively.

We walked along for a while, looking in the store windows and stopping now and then to talk to friends from school.

"Where's Jamie?" asked Kristin Bergner when she and Amy Hamilton walked up to us in front of a frozen-yogurt stand. "I thought she was going to come out with you guys today."

"Yeah, we thought she was coming with us, too," said Lisa. "She said she'd meet us at the front entrance at eight o'clock, but she didn't show."

"Are you sure that you two haven't seen her wandering around the mall looking for us?" I asked. "I'd feel awful if she's here and she thinks we deserted her."

"No," said Kristin, shaking her head. "But if we see her, we'll tell her you're looking for her."

"Thanks," I said, feeling better.

We had only gone a little farther when we heard the sound of running behind us.

"Hey, Eric. Wait up."

I turned around and saw a group of boys from our school hurrying along behind us. They stopped by the pet-shop window, and one of them, Aaron Stemple, was motioning for Eric to come over and talk to them.

Eric gave me an apologetic shrug and sauntered over to them.

Apparently Lisa and Shannon hadn't noticed and were heading on down the walkway. I hesitated. Maybe I should go with them and let Eric catch up. Still, I really liked being with him. I decided to stick around for a couple of minutes and see if he was coming with us or if he would decide to hang out with the other boys.

I glanced over at the guys. They must have told

Eric something really funny, because all of them were laughing their heads off.

I pretended to be interested in something in the window of a camera store. I could see Eric and the boys' reflection in the window. They were still talking and laughing like crazy.

My friends had disappeared in the crowd by now, and I was beginning to think that Eric was going to stay with the guys.

I moved slowly away from the camera shop, still not certain what to do. Eric was so cute, and I didn't have that many chances to be around him outside of school. Still, I didn't want to lose Lisa and Shannon in the crowd either.

Suddenly I remembered Jamie again. I felt awful. She was one of my best friends. What if she really was here, and she thought we were avoiding her?

Maybe I should go looking for her, I thought. But what would I say to her if I found her? *"Gosh, Jamie, there you are. We forgot all about you. Are you having fun in the new mall?"*

Of course not. That would sound dumb.

As I stood there, staring blankly in a swim-shop window, I had the strange feeling that someone was watching me. The swim shop was called Mermaid Magic. Was there someone inside who was staring out at me? A clerk or someone?

I peered through the display. The store was

crowded, and everyone inside appeared to be busy. No one was looking at me. I must have imagined it.

I glanced closer at the scene in the window. Several mannequins wearing gorgeous bikinis were standing around on a fake beach while other mannequins in swimsuits sat in the sand.

Suddenly I knew who was watching me. My mouth went dry. I tried to move away from the window, but I couldn't.

Staring out at me from the swim shop's display was a mannequin.

A mannequin that looked exactly like Jamie!

Chapter

7

It was incredible. The mannequin had the same white-blond hair as Jamie. And even though it was a wig, it was styled in the same short cut that Jamie wore. The eyes were the same, too. Big and blue. But most incredible of all was the face. It was identical to Jamie's face.

I shuddered. That expressionless plastic face seemed to be following my every movement!

Just then I remembered Eric. I glanced quickly over my shoulder. He was still standing there with the guys. I couldn't let him see me freak out over a mannequin. But I wanted to get out of there—fast.

I turned around again, trying to act cool.

"I'm going to go ahead and find Shannon and Lisa," I called to him. "You can catch up. Okay?"

"Sure. See you around," Eric called back.

I ran off down the hall, dodging people and

31

looking for a familiar face. That mannequin had really shaken me up, and I was suddenly uncomfortable being alone, even in such a big crowd. Where could Lisa and Shannon have gone so quickly? I had been waiting for Eric for only a couple of minutes.

A sea of heads bobbed in front of me. But none of them looked familiar. My friends had disappeared.

Up ahead I saw a fudge shop and heard a loud gong. I had been in a fudge shop before and knew that the gong meant a new batch of fudge was about to be poured out on a marble countertop. It also meant free samples. That had to be where my friends were. Especially Lisa. She would do anything for free food.

"Shannon! Lisa!" I called out as I pushed my way into the throng of people crowding toward the counter and the free fudge. "Are you in here, guys?"

A skinny man with a scraggly ponytail and an earring dangling from one ear came up to me. "You rang?" he asked, grinning. "My name's Shannon. What can you do for me?" He snapped his fingers and gazed off into space as if he heard music.

"Uh, wrong Shannon," I mumbled, and ducked out of the shop. What a weirdo!

I looked in a couple of other stores, but no Lisa

or Shannon. I was beginning to feel annoyed. Why hadn't they noticed that I wasn't with them anymore? How come they hadn't come back to find me?

I rode the escalator back down to the main level, thinking maybe they had gone to the food court. Lisa was always starving, and she had wanted to go there when we first got to the mall this morning.

I fished around in my jeans pockets for my map, but I couldn't find it. I must have lost it, but I knew that the food court was somewhere on the main level.

I hurried along, not really paying attention to where I was going. I couldn't get the picture of the mannequin that looked like Jamie out of my mind. The thought of those plastic eyes staring at me made me shudder. Still, it had to be a big coincidence, I reassured myself. She had probably stayed home today and had forgotten to call any of us and tell us. Maybe she had a cold or something.

I suddenly realized that I was in a dark hallway. I hadn't noticed turning into it, and I stopped and peered ahead through the shadows. It was a little spooky, and I started to turn around.

Just then a woman hurried past me in clicky high heels. As soon as she disappeared down the dimly lit hall, I heard a door close.

The rest room! I thought. Maybe that's where

my friends were. It made sense. Shannon and Lisa had probably ducked in to brush their hair and primp in front of the mirror. I might even find Jamie there.

I headed down the hall at a jog. When I reached the door, I started to push it open.

At that instant a pair of hands clamped my shoulders. Someone was grabbing me from behind!

Chapter

opened my mouth and tried to scream, but nothing came out. Just then laughter rang in my ears and filled the dark corridor.

As quickly as they had grabbed me, the hands dropped from my shoulders, and I slowly turned around to face Lisa and Shannon, giggling hysterically.

"You look like you've seen a *ghost!*" said Shannon between giggles.

I was still too shaky to speak, so I glared at her.

"We've been following you ever since you stopped to wait for Eric," bragged Lisa.

"Yeah, we know a secret. You like Eric Sandifer," said Shannon in a singsong voice.

I felt my face turning red. "I do not!" I lied.

"Then why is your face red?" asked Shannon, giggling again.

"So what was the big idea of following me?" I asked, trying to change the subject.

"For fun," said Lisa. "You almost spotted us a couple of times."

"We had to duck into stores," said Shannon.

I turned to Shannon and said, "I suppose this was your idea." She was really getting on my nerves.

"Naturally," said Shannon. She grinned and then bowed like an actress getting a standing ovation. "And it was worth it to see the look on your face."

You should find out how it feels sometime, I thought. *I almost had a heart attack.*

I didn't appreciate Shannon's stupid joke. But mostly I was upset because they knew about my crush on Eric. It was embarrassing for them to know I had a crush on someone who thought of me only as a friend.

"Come on, guys," Shannon said. "We're wasting valuable time that we could be using to shop."

"Or eat," Lisa added emphatically. "Isn't anyone hungry yet? I'm starved."

As if on cue, my stomach growled loudly. We all started laughing. That broke the tension, and we were friends again.

Back out in the main part of the mall we sauntered along arm in arm, heading in the general direction of the food court. We made slow progress, though, because we couldn't resist stopping to check out great-looking clothes in shops along the way.

"Everything's too expensive," I grumbled as we came out of a store called Junior Jungle. It carried only junior sizes and was decorated in a jungle theme with fake monkeys hanging from fake palm trees.

"Tell me about it," said Shannon. "I absolutely have to have a new pair of jeans, and I haven't seen one pair yet that I can afford."

"Why don't you look in Zimmer's?" I suggested. We were walking past the department store, which had jeans of every style and color displayed in its window.

"Great idea," said Shannon. She made a quick left turn into the store. "Anybody want to come with me?"

"I think I'll check the shoe department," said Lisa, hurrying into Zimmer's after her. "I need new tennis shoes. Are you coming, Robin?"

I hung back. I could have used some new tennis shoes, too, but I kept thinking about the mannequin that looked so much like Jamie. I wanted to look at it again—alone.

"No, I need to find the rest room," I lied. "I'll be back in a few minutes."

As I rode the escalator up to the second level and Mermaid Magic, I tried to figure out what I would do if I still thought the dummy looked like

Jamie. I couldn't explain it, even to myself, but I could sense something sinister about that mannequin. I didn't want to tell my friends about it yet. They would think I was nuts.

It probably doesn't look like her at all, I reasoned. I must have been so worried about her not showing up that I only imagined it.

But as I approached the store window, I could see that I had been right the first time. The mannequin really did look just like Jamie.

I tried to look away, but something held me. It was the eyes. I had thought their gaze was blank when I had looked at them before. But now they seemed different. Hard. Angry. Glaring.

Where's Jamie? I wanted to shout at the mannequin. *Why are you here at the mall and she isn't?*

I shuddered. This mannequin couldn't possibly have anything to do with my friend.

But where had it come from? And where was Jamie?

Suddenly my heart stopped.

The mannequin standing next to Jamie was *moving.*

Chapter

I gasped and whirled away from the window. The mannequin's arm had been turned upward at the elbow. Now it had dropped to the mannequin's side.

It couldn't have possibly happened.

But I had seen it.

Just chill out, I ordered myself, and purposely walked away from Mermaid Magic without looking back.

So what if I thought I saw a mannequin's hand move? A customer probably bumped against it. Plastic dummies don't move by themselves. And so what if the store had a mannequin that looked like Jamie? And its eyes gave me the creeps? It was only a coincidence. That's all. It's silly to get all freaked out over a couple of mannequins.

Shannon and Lisa were waiting for me outside

the department store when I got back. Neither of them carried any packages.

"What's the matter?" I asked. "Couldn't you find anything you liked?"

"Too expensive," Lisa said.

"How about you, Shannon?" I asked. "You must have been able to find a pair of jeans in there."

"None that I really liked," she said. "Come on, guys. Let's get something to eat."

I shrugged and walked along with the others to the food court. With all the shops and cool things to buy I hated to spend money on food. But I was definitely getting hungry. In fact, my stomach was growling so loudly at one point that a man walking in front of me had actually turned around and looked at me.

"Why don't we see a movie?" suggested Lisa, dragging a french fry through a blob of ketchup a few minutes later. "I've been smelling the popcorn all morning."

"Don't you ever think about anything but food?" I teased.

Lisa pretended to look hurt. Then she grinned slyly and said, "I thought it might help me keep my mind off those diamonds in that jewelry-store window over there. I'm just dying to buy some earrings and maybe a tiara or two."

I looked toward the jewelry-store window,

where a mannequin head modeled a brilliant diamond necklace, matching earrings, and a ruby-and-emerald tiara.

"I see exactly what you mean, dahling," I said, speaking with a bogus English accent. "It's a *terrible* temptation."

Giggling, we dumped our lunch trash into a bin and headed for the lobby of Cinema Six to study the posters of the six movies playing. There were a couple of sappy-looking romances, a cop movie, a horror flick, a cartoon, and a comedy. After a lot of discussion we finally settled on the comedy and bought our tickets.

"We have forty-five minutes until the movie starts," said Shannon. "Let's kill some time by looking in a couple more stores."

"You're kidding, right?" I groaned. "After paying for lunch and a movie ticket, I can't even afford to window-shop!"

The department store at this end of the mall was called Stryker's, and I could see right away that it was a lot less expensive than Zimmer's. My friends and I split up, and I made a beeline for the jewelry department.

I looked at earrings for a while. I didn't see anything that I liked all that much, so I went to find my friends. Walking past the young men's department, I glanced toward the dressing-room area. That's not something I usually do. I mean, I wasn't trying to see guys without clothes on or anything. I guess something just attracted my attention.

I looked again and then stopped in my tracks. One of the dressing-room stall doors was partway open, and a mannequin was standing in front of the mirror. Or was it a mannequin? The body looked like an ordinary mannequin, but the head seemed wrong. There was definitely something weird about the head.

I squinted and looked again. Above the stiff, shiny vinyl body was the head of a teenage boy.

His eyes were open wide, and his mouth was moving!

He was alive!

Chapter

I closed my eyes and shook my head in disbelief. When I opened them again, a salesclerk with a long black French braid was standing right outside the dressing room. She was glaring at me, and when she saw me looking back, she quickly closed the stall door.

She knows I saw him! I thought in a panic. *And now she's guarding the door. This is ridiculous,* I scolded myself. *There's no such thing as half mannequin and half person. I must be going berserk.*

I pretended to be looking at some merchandise while I tried to get a grip on myself. I must have been standing there five minutes before I realized that I was in the little boys' department.

So what, I thought with a defiant toss of my

head. *I could be shopping for my little brother—
if I had one.*

Finally the salesclerk with the long black French braid went off to help a customer. I glanced at the dressing-room door. It was still closed.

I had to know what was inside. I crept closer. The young men's department was practically deserted. No one would notice if I quickly opened the door and peeked inside.

Besides, if I got caught, I could always say I was looking for my brother.

All the other stall doors were open in the dressing-room area. At least no one would come popping out of a stall and start asking a lot of embarrassing questions.

I closed my hand around the doorknob and slowly turned it. Then I eased the door open with my foot. I jumped with a start as the mannequin came into view, and then I collapsed with relief when I saw that it was only a mannequin.

A plain old dummy with a plastic body and a plastic head. I stared at it for a moment. I had been crazy to think its mouth was moving.

I turned to walk away when something about the mannequin made me stop. I didn't know what it was, but something wasn't quite right. I had to look closer.

The dummy looked like one of the boys Eric had been talking to a little while ago. The long thin nose. The dark unruly hair. Even the Pittsburgh Steelers sweatshirt was familiar.

The mannequin *did* look like one of Eric's friends.

It looked *exactly* like Aaron Stemple!

Chapter

11

backed slowly away from the dressing room, keeping my eyes fastened on the dummy's face. I had to show someone. *Fast.*

Turning around, I broke into a run, zigzagging through the clothing displays. Shannon and Lisa were somewhere in this store. But where? *Jeans, maybe,* I thought. *Or shoes.*

"Robin!"

I screeched to a stop at the sound of my name and whirled around. It was Eric, and he was jogging toward me through the racks of sport shirts with a big grin on his face.

I was too frightened even to notice whether or not there was a dimple in his chin.

"What's happening?" he asked.

"Come on! You've got to see this!" I cried in a high-pitched voice I hardly recognized as mine. "I think I'm going crazy!"

I grabbed him by the arm and pulled him toward the young men's department.

"You're acting totally bizarre, Robin," he said in a puzzled voice. "What's wrong?"

"It's Aaron. You know. Aaron Stemple," I stammered. "You were just talking to him, right?"

Eric frowned. "Yeah, sure. What about Aaron? Did he get hurt or something?"

"Just hurry!" I insisted.

Half dragging Eric behind me, I marched straight into the dressing-room area and headed toward the stall where I'd seen the mannequin.

"Hey, wait a minute!" cried Eric. "You can't go in there. That's where *guys* change."

"It doesn't matter," I said, still charging full speed ahead.

I grabbed the knob and jerked the door open.

"Hey! Get outta here!"

I had walked in on a good-looking blond teenage boy, trying on clothes. He was clutching a pair of jeans in front of him and staring at me with bugged-out eyes.

Heat raced up my neck and turned my cheeks bright pink as I stared back at him. "I—I—"

"Geez, Robin, I told you that you couldn't come in here," Eric said from behind me. I could tell from the sound of his voice that he was almost as embarrassed as I was. "Come on. Let's get out of here before they call security."

There was nothing in the world that I wanted to do more than turn around and run away from the half-naked boy. But I had to know about Aaron.

"Excuse me," I said, being careful to keep my eyes on the boy's face. "Could you tell me if there was a mannequin in here when you came in?"

"What!" he shrieked.

"Have you completely lost it?" Eric cried.

He grabbed my arm and tried to pull me away, but I wouldn't budge.

"Well? Was there?" I pressed. "Right here in this dressing room. A dummy with dark hair and a Pittsburgh Steelers sweatshirt. I have to know!"

"The only dummy around here is you!" the boy said angrily. "Now get outta here."

"Come on, Robin," said Eric, pulling my arm again.

This time I didn't resist.

When we got outside the dressing-room area, Eric gave me a disgusted look and walked away.

"Listen, Eric, you've got to believe me," I said, hurrying after him. "It looked exactly like Aaron. I swear."

Eric stopped and glared over his shoulder at me. "Look, Robin, I saw Aaron about twenty minutes ago, and he was a perfectly normal kid," he said angrily. "No plastic skin. No glassy eyes. Just a kid. Got that?"

"But do you know where he is now?" I asked quickly.

"Sure. In the arcade, playing video games."

"Do you know *for sure* that he's in there?" I pressed.

"That's where he was heading, okay?" He shook his head in amazement. "When you said you were going crazy, you hit it right on the nose."

"Eric, listen to me," I said. "I don't care what you think about me, just find Aaron. I've got to make sure he's okay."

"Find him yourself," he said, and walked away.

Chapter

12

I watched him go with a lump in my throat. I had never felt so alone in my life. Eric didn't believe a word I had said. In fact, he was convinced that I had come totally unglued.

Maybe he was right. No sane person could possibly believe that human beings could turn into mannequins.

But I had seen it with my own eyes.

"Hey, Robin. There you are. We've been looking all over for you."

Lisa and Shannon were rushing toward me.

"Where have you been?" Shannon asked. "It's almost time for the movie to start."

I glanced down at my watch, hoping they wouldn't notice how shook up I was.

"I've been looking for you, too," I said. Then I got an idea. "We've still got ten minutes. Come on, there's something I want to show you guys."

"Sure. What is it?" asked Lisa.

"Come with me and find out," I said, trying my best to sound mysterious.

It worked, because they practically fell all over themselves following me up the escalator to the second level.

I was heading for Mermaid Magic. I would lead them up to the window display and wait for their reaction. If they didn't notice the mannequin and say it looked like Jamie, then I would know that I had imagined everything. But if they did see Jamie's face in that plastic one, I would tell them about Aaron. Then we could go to the arcade and look for him together.

The second floor of the mall was less crowded than the main level, and I could see the window display when we were three stores away. I frowned. Who was that person moving around inside?

"Oh, no!" I whispered. "They're changing the display!"

I dashed ahead of my friends, stopping outside the window and doing a double take. A teenage girl was arranging new mannequins on the fake beach. I had seen her before. She was the clerk with the black French braid who worked in Stryker's. The one who had closed the dressing-room door when I thought I had spotted a mannequin with a live boy's head—Aaron's head.

My mind was racing. *What's she doing here? And where's the mannequin that looks like Jamie?*

Just as my friends came up beside me, the clerk picked up a mannequin from the floor behind her and walked toward the back of the store. It was the Jamie-mannequin!

Pushing Lisa and Shannon aside, I raced into Mermaid Magic after her.

"Stop!" I shouted. "Bring that mannequin back!"

The clerk with the French braid didn't even hesitate. She marched straight to a door that was marked Storage and pushed it open.

"Please, miss," I called in desperation. "Please wait a minute. I need to see that mannequin. It's important!"

Still ignoring me, she went inside the storage room and slammed the door in my face.

Lisa was the first to catch up with me, and she touched my shoulder gently and said, "Robin, what are you doing? What's the matter with you?"

"Yeah, how come you're weirding out?" Shannon added.

"I'm not weirding out," I snapped. Then I turned back to the storage-room door and pounded on it with my fist. "Open this door and let me in!" I shouted. "Open it right now!"

"I'm sorry," came an icy voice from the other side of the panel. "Only authorized personnel are allowed in this room."

At that moment something seemed to burst inside me, and I started crying hysterically. "You can't do this!" I sobbed. "I want *Jamie* back! I want *Jamie* back! I want *Jamie* . . . *Jamie* . . . *Jamie* . . ."

Chapter

"Robin! It's okay!" Shannon said, pulling me away from the storage-room door.

"Shh. Don't cry," soothed Lisa. "Everything's going to be all right."

My friends clustered around me. I buried my face in Shannon's shoulder, feeling grateful that they were there. But my mind was still swirling, and I knew I wasn't making much sense.

"It was Jamie . . . she was in the window . . . but she wasn't real . . . she was a mannequin," I babbled uncontrollably. "And then there's Aaron . . . Aaron Stemple . . . his head was alive. . . ."

"Come on, Robin. Let's go back down to the food court and get you something cold to drink," urged Shannon. She put an arm around me and led me toward the door.

I started to go with her and then stopped.

55

"But the mannequin," I said stubbornly. "You *have* to see it."

"We'll see it later," Lisa assured me. "Right now we need to go down to the food court."

"You can tell us all about it there," said Shannon. "Here, take this tissue."

I thanked her for the tissue and blew my nose. I knew that my eyes were red and puffy. Who cared? What was important was that the clerk with the black French braid had been carrying Jamie away!

But that wasn't Jamie, I reminded myself. *It was a mannequin. One who* looked *like Jamie,* I thought, my mind reeling in total confusion.

Suddenly I had the creepy feeling that someone was watching me. Had the clerk with the French braid followed me to the food court?

Slowly I raised my eyes and looked around, abruptly coming face-to-face with Kitty Lopez and Diane Davies at a nearby table. They were both in my gym class and were the biggest gossips in school. I felt my face turning red as I realized that they had probably seen me crying. I would die if they came over and asked what was wrong.

The moment my eyes met theirs, they looked away from me and started talking and giggling together. *They're probably talking about me!* I thought angrily.

By the time we had finished our drinks, Kitty and Diane had left the food court, and I had calmed down and told Lisa and Shannon about both of the mannequins. I left out the part about Eric and me walking into the dressing room where the boy was changing clothes.

That was too embarrassing to tell even my best friends about.

"Wow," said Shannon, shaking her head in amazement when I had stopped talking. "What a story."

"You can say that again," said Lisa. "Now let me see if I've got this straight. You want us to believe that there is a mannequin that looks exactly like Jamie, and that it's been standing in the window at Mermaid Magic and staring at you whenever you stopped by. You also want us to believe you saw Aaron Stemple being turned into a mannequin in the young men's department of Stryker's Department Store."

I could see that she thought I was crazy, too. "Well, if that boggles your mind, listen to this," I said sarcastically. "That same salesclerk—the one with the black French braid who was carrying Jamie away—was working in Stryker's guarding the dressing room where Aaron was." I sat back in my chair and looked at them defiantly.

No one said anything for a moment.

Finally Lisa sighed deeply and said, "I know you think those things really happened, but you're so upset over Jamie not showing up today that you're not making sense. You're imagining things."

I knew I wasn't getting anywhere, so I decided to play along. "You're probably right," I murmured. "I guess when I saw that mannequin that looked so much like Jamie, I kind of lost it."

We sat there for a little while longer watching the shoppers go by. Finally Shannon jumped up.

"Eeek, we forgot all about the movie," she said. "It's almost half-over."

"Oh, no." I groaned. It was my fault. "I'm sorry, guys. I really am. Come on, let's see if we can turn in our tickets and get our money back."

"We could hang around for the next showing," offered Lisa.

"Naw," said Shannon. "I'm not really interested in seeing a movie anymore."

"Me, either," I said. Then another idea hit me. "After we stop by the ticket booth, we can go to the arcade and see if any cute boys are playing video games."

"What you mean is, see if Eric Sandifer's playing video games," Shannon said slyly.

Lisa giggled. "You can't fool us. We know you have a crush on Eric."

I smiled to myself. *Let them think that if they want to,* I thought. Of course, it was true that I had a crush on Eric, but more important, it was my chance to look for Aaron Stemple.

Chapter

When we asked for our money back, the boy in the ticket booth at Cinema Six shrugged and said, "Your tickets are still good. Just go on in."

"We don't want to go on in," argued Lisa. "The movie already started."

"It hasn't been on that long," he said.

"Yes, it has," I fired back. "We've missed the entire beginning."

He heaved a sigh and looked from one of us to the other. He was sort of good-looking, with an athletic build and wavy dark hair. He was wearing a T-shirt that said PROPERTY OF THE NEW YORK YANKEES.

"So?" the guy said. "When it's over, just stay in your seats. When it starts again, you can watch the stuff you missed. Like I said, go ahead. Go on in."

"We don't *want* to do that," said Shannon. "We've changed our minds. You couldn't *pay* us to sit through that movie."

"Hey, you'd really love this flick. A million laughs. I'm serious. Check it out." When we didn't answer, he bent closer to the opening in the booth's window and whispered, "What's the matter? Afraid of the dark?"

Lisa's eyes flared angrily. "Our money, please," she said, holding out her hand. "And hurry up with it."

The boy shrugged and exchanged our tickets for cash. "Boy, was he ever pushy," said Lisa as we moved out into the mall again.

"Yeah," I grumbled. "He really wanted us to go in that theater. Afraid of the dark! Huh! What a bozo."

Shannon shrugged. "Maybe the manager doesn't like it when he refunds people's money."

By now we could see the arcade. It was just ahead on the left. The closer I got to it, the more nervous I became.

"I sure hope Aaron's in there," I muttered, not realizing I had said it out loud.

"Aaron?" Lisa said in surprise. "I thought you liked Eric."

"I do, but—" I broke off, realizing what I had admitted. "Come on, guys. Give me a break. I need to find out if Aaron's okay, or if he's . . . well, you know."

"We know. A mannequin," scoffed Shannon, rolling her eyes. "You guys can go to the arcade if you want to, but I'm going into that western-wear store over there. I want to check out their jeans. Lisa, want to come with me?"

Lisa threw me a guilty look and said, "Sure. I could use some new jeans, too."

"Go ahead, think I'm crazy. That's okay. I'll go to the arcade by myself," I said, sighing. "And I'll meet you two right here in ten minutes."

Stepping out of the bright lights of the mall, I needed a minute for my eyes to adjust to the darkness inside the arcade.

The rows of video machines shot out bursts of ear-splitting noises. Eerie lights bathed the faces of the players in ghostly colors.

I started up and down the rows of machines, stopping first at a game called Dueling Gangsters, where twenties-style gangsters jumped out of hiding places and shot machine guns at each other with loud rat-a-tat-tats. A girl was playing that game, so I moved on.

There were groups of cheering boys and girls clustered around the players at every set of controls. Once I thought I saw Aaron at Monsters of the Catacomb, but when I got closer, it wasn't him. Then I spotted a boy in a Steelers sweatshirt playing a martial arts game called Shadow Ninjas, but that wasn't Aaron either.

"Want to get in on the action, miss?" a voice asked. "I can set you up on The Haunted Shopping Mall back in the corner." I felt a tap on my shoulder.

I jumped a mile and turned around. "The haunted shop—" I started to say, and froze.

The teenage boy standing there was exactly the same person who had refunded our money at Cinema Six not five minutes before!

The only thing different about him was that now he was wearing a T-shirt with Wonderland Mall Arcade printed across the front.

My mind was spinning again. This was the third salesclerk that had reappeared at different stores all over the mall. What was going on?

"But . . . you . . . ," I stammered.

"It's a great game," he urged, motioning for me to come with him. His eyes glowed red in the reflected lights from the machines. "But it's back in the corner where kids hardly ever notice it. Come on. You can play the first time free." There was something about the way he said the words that made me shiver. It was almost as if he were daring me to play the game.

The one back in the corner.

That kids hardly ever noticed.

Called The Haunted Shopping Mall!

Chapter

15

"Can't. I'm in a hurry," I said. "I'm looking for somebody. Maybe you've seen him. He's got dark hair and he's wearing a Steelers sweatshirt."

The boy didn't say anything for a moment. He just stared at me with those blood-red eyes. Finally his gaze flickered and he said, "Oh, yeah. I remember him. He was here, but he left."

"When?" I asked quickly.

The boy shrugged. "I dunno. Five minutes ago. Ten, maybe."

"Thanks," I said. "I have to find him."

I started to leave, but he reached out, stopping me. He bent closer, cupping his hand near my ear as if he were going to tell me a secret.

"Sure you won't play the game?" he asked in a whisper. "It's free. It won't cost you a penny."

Then he looked deep into my eyes again. The red glow seemed to be slowly spreading from his eyes to cover his entire face.

I suddenly felt weak and a little dizzy. I wanted to look away, but I couldn't. It was as if I was paralyzed by his gaze.

I knew my feet were on the ground, but it felt as if I were floating. Floating toward two points of blazing red light. The whole world was turning red as I floated closer.

And closer.

Chapter

16

felt as if I were drifting into the sun. The heat was incredible. The light was blinding me. I was powerless to fight it. And yet, I didn't even want to fight it. I wanted to drift on . . . and on . . . and on.

Suddenly I was aware of movement in my line of vision. I squinted into the brightness. I could make out a form. A small form. It seemed to be a little girl, and she had darted in between the boy and me and was tugging on his arm.

"Hey, mister," the little girl said. "Got change for a dollar?"

"No change," he growled, and shot her an angry look.

The instant he glanced away from me, the spell was broken. The weakness I'd felt was gone, and strength surged back into me. I was firmly on the ground again. Putting one foot carefully behind the other one, I cautiously backed toward the door.

"Wait!" he shouted. "The free game. Don't you want to play?"

"No, thanks," I muttered, bolting out of the arcade as fast as I could.

Out in the mall again, I was panting so hard I could barely breathe. I had to find Shannon and Lisa and get out of there. As much as I wanted to head straight to the exit, I couldn't leave them. I didn't know what was happening, but something terrible was going on at Wonderland Mall. We were all in danger.

Shannon and Lisa weren't waiting at the spot we'd agreed on, so I headed toward the western-wear store at a run. Maybe they had gotten carried away trying on jeans and were still inside.

I stopped at the entrance of the store and scanned the showroom. I sighed with relief. There was Shannon, talking to a clerk.

I started toward her and stopped. The clerk had her back to me, so her face was hidden. But she had blond hair cascading over her shoulders, and she was wearing a miniskirt and a sweater!

Fear clogged my throat. I tried to call out a warning to Shannon to get away from that clerk as fast as she could. But the only sound I could get out was a croak.

"Oh, there you are, Robin. I thought we were

supposed to meet out in the mall."

It was Lisa, and I gulped in some air and turned around, still trying to speak.

"I didn't see anything I liked in here," she was saying, "so I tried another place a couple of doors down. They had the most adorable . . ."

Suddenly her mouth dropped open and her face went pale. She was staring over my shoulder. She must have seen something happening behind me. Behind me where Shannon and the girl with the blond hair were.

"Oh, no!" She gasped and clutched my arm. "Robin, *look*! It's Shannon!"

I glanced back at Shannon. She was gazing intently at the clerk, a soft smile on her face as if she'd just seen something very pleasant. But then she began to change. Behind her wire-rimmed glasses her eyes took on a look of alarm. She seemed to be trying to cry out, but her lips barely moved. No sound came out! Shannon grabbed wildly at the clerk, but her arm made only a jerky motion and then grew stiff, stopping halfway out in the air. And her skin took on a plasticlike shine.

I couldn't move. My worst nightmare had come true.

Shannon Markoff had been turned into a mannequin right before my eyes!

Chapter

"We've got to get out of here!" I cried.

"I can't believe it. It's not possible," Lisa murmured. "It looked like . . ." She didn't finish her sentence. She just stared at me as if the whole thing was too much to comprehend.

"Believe it, Lisa," I said. "I know it's not possible, but that clerk turned Shannon into a mannequin!" I could hear the panic in my own voice. "What have I been telling you? Come on, Lisa. Let's go before the same thing happens to *us*!"

I tugged on her arm, but she didn't move. "I want to go, too. Really," she whispered. "But we can't leave Shannon here."

"She's a *mannequin*!" I insisted. "You didn't believe me at first. You thought I was making the whole thing up about Jamie and Aaron. But now you've seen it with your own eyes."

"This is crazy," Lisa said, shaking her head. "It can't be happening. We've got to go into that store and find out for sure if that mannequin is really Shannon. I mean, maybe we just imagined it. Or it's a coincidence that the mannequin looks so much like Shannon. It *could* happen that way, you know." She didn't sound as if she believed what she was saying herself.

"No! No!" I shrieked. "You saw it happen. You know it's her."

"I know it looks like her from a distance," Lisa reasoned. "And I know it's wearing glasses like hers. But what if Shannon accidentally dropped her glasses, and a salesclerk found them and put them on the mannequin as a joke? And we're so paranoid that we thought that mannequin was a real person when we first got here?"

"Lisa, listen to me, you can't go back in there," I begged. She wasn't listening, though. She had brushed past me and was heading into the store.

I ran after her. I had to tell her about the boy in the video arcade and his blood-red eyes and hypnotizing gaze.

Lisa must have known I was following her, because she was moving awfully fast. The store was larger than I had thought when I first looked inside, and the mannequin Lisa was heading toward was near the back.

"Wait a minute," I called to her. "I'm coming, too."

She let me catch up, but she didn't look at me. She was staring at the display containing the mannequin. Her mouth was open, and her eyes bulged wide.

"Look," she whispered, her voice quivering. "It *is* Shannon. And look at the mannequin standing beside her. It's *Jamie*. Oh, Robin, I'm scared! What are we going to do?"

Just then I heard someone come up behind us.

"May I help you girls find something to try on?"

The blonde in the miniskirt stood between us and the door.

Chapter

"Um . . . we're about to leave, thanks," I said, and swallowed hard. Little icicles of fear raced up my back.

I moved away from the mannequins and pretended to be looking at a western shirt with fringe across the front. I kept my head bent toward the merchandise, but my eyes were searching the room, looking for the fastest route to the door.

"We have some terrific opening-day sales," said the girl, moving closer. "Maybe you'd like to try something on. I'd be glad to show you to the dressing rooms."

I exchanged terrified glances with Lisa.

"We'll let you know if we find something," I said stiffly. "Come on, Lisa, let's look over here."

My heart was pounding as I motioned for her to follow me. I knew we had to get out of the store, but I was afraid to make any sudden moves. I didn't know what the blonde might do. I decided that our best bet was to keep pretending to look at clothes and gradually make our way toward the front of the store and the door.

Suddenly I realized that it had gotten deathly still. I glanced around. Lisa and I were the only customers in the place. There had been lots of people browsing among the merchandise a few minutes ago. Now there weren't even any other salesclerks around.

It was then I realized that mannequins were all over the store. There were displays of mannequins roping fake cows and riding fake horses. Others were showing off elaborate pairs of cowboy boots. I had never seen so many dummies modeling clothing in one store before in my life. My heart was in my throat. I moved closer to Lisa.

She was standing in front of a pair of mannequins, staring at them intently.

I glanced at them, too. One was wearing an oversize sleep-shirt with a cartoon character of a horse in a cowboy hat on the front. The other one had on pajamas.

Lisa squeezed my hand and whispered, "Doesn't the one in the sleep-shirt remind you of a girl in our social-studies class?"

I squinted and looked at it again. She was right. I didn't know the girl's name, but she was short and really overweight. So was the mannequin.

I caught my breath. Who had ever heard of a short, fat mannequin! But then, who had ever heard of a mannequin wearing wire-rimmed glasses? Or having the face of someone I knew?

I looked slowly around the store, gazing at first one mannequin and then another. A lot of the faces were familiar. Kids from classes. Kids I saw in the halls. And every one of them was frozen into the form of a mannequin.

I started edging toward the door again, moving more quickly this time.

"Lisa, we've got to get out of here right now," I mumbled. "Before it's too late."

As I moved, I tried to keep as far away from the mannequins as possible. On all sides of me mannequins smiled at me with painted smiles, their eyes following me as I went past. Had some of them moved? Reached out hands as I went by? I didn't dare look back to find out.

Hurry! Hurry! I screamed inside my head.

The blonde was blocking the door. She didn't say anything. She just smiled and looked at us with her enormous blue eyes.

As much as I tried not to, I couldn't help looking back. And then I forgot about wanting to leave the store. Her eyes were so big and so blue that it was like looking into the sea. So peaceful. Like riding a raft away from the beach. Bobbing along in the gentle waves. Feeling the warmth of the sun. Wanting to stay there forever.

Suddenly something clicked inside my brain. This peaceful, drifting feeling was the same sensation I'd had in the arcade when I had looked into that boy's blood-red eyes. *Danger! Danger!* The words flashed like a strobe light in my brain.

"Lisa! Don't look at her eyes!" I shouted, clamping my own eyes shut. "That's how they do it! With their eyes!"

Chapter

Grabbing Lisa's hand, I pulled her away from the clerk. We ducked low and zigzagged through racks of clothing and behind display cases as we made a mad dash toward the back of the store.

"Where are you going?" Lisa called in a hoarse whisper. "We'll be trapped in here with that . . . monster!"

"I see a door back here," I whispered back. "It's our only chance."

"Girls! Girls, where are you?" The clerk's voice rang out in the silent store.

We froze behind a rack of skirts. My heart was pounding so loudly, I was sure she could hear it. Lisa's face was frozen in a look of pure terror.

"It won't do you any good to try to hide," the

blonde said. Her voice was soft and coaxing now. "I've closed the door to the mall and locked it. The three of us are all alone in the store," she purred. "It's only a matter of time until I find you. And I will find you."

I tried to swallow, but I couldn't. I held my breath, listening for what she would do next.

Suddenly there was a racket near the front of the store.

I raised my head and peered over the skirts. Her back was to us, and she was furiously pulling garments off the racks and dumping over display cases. The air was filled with the screech of hangers being raked across rods and with the sound of shattering glass.

She wasn't coaxing anymore. Her mood had changed. She was destroying the entire store in her frantic search for us!

"I'm going to find you!" she raged. "I'm going to get you!"

"Now!" I whispered to Lisa. "While she's looking the other way."

We dashed toward the door. What if it was locked? Where else could we go? The blond girl would have us cornered. We'd be goners.

I grabbed the knob and turned it. It was open! I pulled the door open enough for us to squeeze through and closed it securely behind us.

"Lock it!" urged Lisa.

"I can't!" I whispered frantically. "It doesn't have a lock!"

"Oh, my gosh! When she can't find us out there, she's bound to come in here," said Lisa.

My eyes darted around the room. No windows. No way out. It was just a small, cramped store-room filled with boxes and boxes of merchandise.

"Maybe we could hide in a box," Lisa cried. Her voice was thin and squeaky with fright.

I shook my head. "There has to be a better place."

I slumped against the wall to catch my breath when I heard the blonde screaming again.

"You little brats! Where are you?" Her voice was coming closer. "You can't hide from me! *I'll . . . get . . . you!*"

My blood froze. There had to be a place to hide. There just had to!

"Look!" whispered Lisa. She was pointing to a stack of boxes. The outline of a door showed behind them.

Together we wildly threw the boxes aside. A sign on the door read Freight Entrance. My heart leaped. If we could just get through this door, we could surely find the back entrance to the mall and freedom!

The heavy metal door opened with a heart-wrenching groan. Had the blond girl heard it? There was no time to lose. We propelled ourselves

81

through the opening as it clanged shut behind us.

We were out!

We were free!

Our moment of relief ended abruptly as we looked at our surroundings. Instead of the bright hallway leading to an outdoor loading ramp which we had expected, we were in a dimly lit passageway that slanted downward. A damp, moldy smell hung in the chilly air.

Clutching each other in terror, we crept slowly down the passage toward the dark unknown.

Chapter

Lisa peered fearfully around the passageway. "I don't like this," she said in a breathy whisper. "It's creepy, and I'm scared. I want to go home."

"Me, too," I said. "But you know we can't go back into that store. We don't have any other choice. We have to see where this goes."

It was as silent as a tomb as we crept along in the darkness. Still, I couldn't help glancing back over my shoulder every few steps to see if we were being followed. And I kept picturing Shannon, turning from a happy, smiling girl into a stiff, plastic mannequin with terror-filled eyes. And Aaron, struggling to cry out the instant before he was changed into a lifeless dummy. I couldn't let the same thing happen to Lisa and me—*no matter what.*

Just ahead I spotted another door. It was on the

left side of the hallway, the same side as the door we had come out of.

"Let's try it," I said.

"I don't know," said Lisa, hesitating in front of the door, her face filled with confusion. "What if that blonde is in there waiting for us? She's been showing up in a lot of different places."

And so have the clerk with the French braid and the boy from the movie theater and the video arcade, I thought, but I didn't say it out loud. Somebody had to make decisions, and Lisa was too terrified to make them.

"Maybe it goes into another store, and we can cut through it and get back to the main part of the mall. Then all we have to do is grab the next bus to town, and we're outta here," I said, trying to sound more optimistic than I felt. "Let's try it."

I could tell that Lisa didn't want to do it, but she watched silently as I reached for the doorknob. The door was locked!

"Darn!" I muttered. "Let's keep going. Maybe there's another door up ahead that isn't locked."

"Do we have to?" Lisa's eyes were pleading. "Couldn't we just . . . just . . ."

"Just what? Can't you see that there is nothing else to do?" I insisted.

This time as we moved along, Lisa stayed behind me. Seeing another door on the left, I surged forward.

"Wait for me!" called Lisa, reaching out and grabbing the back of my belt.

That door was locked, too, and the next one, and the next one. And all the time we had been moving downward, deeper and deeper into the dark innards of the mall.

"Robin, look. There's a door on the other side of the hall," Lisa shouted. Her words echoed off the heavy walls. "Maybe it goes to the outside!"

"And home free!" I added, speeding toward it.

Incredibly, the knob turned in my hand. Holding my breath, I inched it open.

Instead of daylight, all I saw was more darkness. My heart sank.

"We aren't outside yet," I said. "But we must be getting closer. Come on."

Lisa was trembling as I dragged her through the door, and she was whimpering softly.

"It'll be okay," I said, but in truth, I wasn't so sure.

Since we had been in the dimly lit passageway for so long, our eyes adjusted quickly to the room we were now in.

Something about it was familiar. I had the eerie feeling that I had been there before. I stared intently into the shadows.

"Oh, no!" I cried.

We were back in the storage room.

The one filled with mannequins.

Chapter

21

Looking around, I realized that there were at least twice as many mannequins in the room now as there had been that morning. They were heaped and piled everywhere. Their arms and legs were bent at odd angles and pointing every which way. Some of their heads lolled to one side or were turned around completely backward.

Lisa grabbed my arm. "Where did they all come from?"

Then, turning her frightened eyes on me, she stammered, "Do you think that they're . . . that they used to be . . . kids . . . like us?"

Or like Jamie. And Shannon, I thought. I didn't answer Lisa. The idea was too awful to think about.

While Lisa cringed by the door, I began walking

slowly among the mannequins. I didn't think I could stand to look at their painted faces, but I had to.

The room was deathly still as I tiptoed across the floor toward a pair of girl mannequins, sitting with their backs propped against the far wall and their legs straight out in front. Their heads were upright, and their blank eyes stared straight ahead. They made me think of puppets whose strings had been cut.

I inched forward, not wanting them to look like anyone I knew, but knowing they would. I stared at them in horror. "Lisa, don't look if you don't want to, but I've found Kitty Lopez and Diane Davies."

I closed my eyes, picturing the two of them looking at me in the food court. I had been so afraid that they would come over and ask what was wrong.

If only they had! I thought. *Maybe I could have warned them!* But deep inside I knew they wouldn't have listened.

"Are you sure it's them?" Lisa asked in a trembling voice.

"Positive," I murmured.

For the first time since I entered the mall that morning, I felt totally helpless. Trapped. And tears of frustration and dread made little rivers down my face. My mind was whirling as I imagined all of these boys and girls, innocently going to a store clerk for help, or to a ticket booth to get into the movies, or to the boy behind the counter in the video arcade for change. And looking into their eyes . . .

Chill out! I ordered myself. *Getting emotional will only make things worse.*

I moved on among the mannequins again, peering into their silent faces. Most of them were strangers, but lots of them weren't. A boy from my language-arts class was crumpled in a corner. Near him was Marti LaMaster, the pitcher on our school's softball team for girls; and Aaron Stemple, still wearing his Steelers sweatshirt, was stretched out on the floor.

"And here's Amy Hamilton and Kristin Bergner," I called to Lisa. "Remember how we saw them a few hours ago and asked them if they'd seen Jamie?"

Lisa nodded and covered her face with her hands. "Don't look anymore, Robin. Please." She sobbed. "I don't want to know who they are. I don't want to become one of them. I just want to go home."

A sudden noise on the other side of the room startled me. There was another door. It looked like the door we had come through when we entered this room earlier in the day. And someone was unlocking it.

Lisa had heard it, too. I signaled her. "Quick! Someone's coming! Lie down on the floor and pretend you're a mannequin!" I whispered.

From the look on her face I knew that she was too terrified to move. Grabbing her shirt, I pulled her down beside me. A second later the door opened.

"Keep your eyes open and try not to breathe," I murmured.

A blinding stab of light was the first thing that came into the room. My head was turned so that I could see the doorway out of the corner of my eye. Someone was coming in.

At first all I could see was a ghostly black silhouette. But as it came closer, I began to make out its features.

It was the girl with the dark French braid!

And she was carrying a mannequin under one arm!

90

Chapter

I wanted to jump up and run screaming from the room. But instead I held my breath and tried with every ounce of strength that I had to keep from trembling.

She was coming closer.

Beside me Lisa's hand moved!

Had the girl with the French braid seen it? I heard her chuckle to herself as she wandered around the room. "You poor kids," she said in a cold, sarcastic voice. "Look at all of you. What a shame you had to be sacrificed."

I thought I was going to faint. What did she mean, *sacrificed*? What had she and the others done to everyone?

The mannequin she was carrying dropped to the floor with a sickening thud. She pushed him aside with her foot as if he were nothing more than a bag of garbage.

My eyes flicked toward him for an instant. It was a boy with red hair, but I couldn't see his face. Frantically I racked my brain. *Do I know any red-haired boys?* I wondered. Right now I was too scared to remember anything.

Why wasn't she leaving? I thought with a jolt. She had pitched another mannequin into this storage room. So why didn't she go back into the mall? Why was she just standing there?

I didn't dare look at her. She might see my eyes move.

But what if she was looking at Lisa and me right now? What if she had noticed that our skin didn't shine like the plastic dummies lying all around us? And that there were no painted smiles on our faces?

Why didn't I remember to smile! I screamed inside my head.

She took another step toward us. And another. And another, until she was standing right beside me. Her feet were pointing to the left side of my head, the toes almost touching my hair. She was so close that I could hear her breathing.

My heart was racing. My lungs were bursting. I desperately needed to gulp in air. Every muscle in my body was screaming to move. *To run.*

Suddenly the door burst open again.

"What's taking you so long?" It was the blond girl in the miniskirt.

I could see her standing in the doorway, her chin raised angrily and her hands clamped against her hips.

"I was dumping another one of the little brats in here," spat out the girl with the French braid.

"Come on. I need you," commanded the blonde. "I had two of them trapped, but they managed to get away."

The girl with the French braid laughed contemptuously. "Not for long, they didn't."

She stomped toward the door in long, determined strides and slammed it behind her, leaving Lisa and me trembling in the dark.

Chapter

At first I couldn't move. Beside me I could hear Lisa crying softly.

"What are they going to do to us?" she said, sobbing. "When we were in the store and the blonde wanted us to try things on, all I did was look at her and I started feeling funny. You said something about her eyes."

I nodded and explained to her about the boy in the video arcade and how his blood-red eyes had put me into a sort of a trance.

"But who are they?" Lisa whispered. "And why are they doing this? Why are they turning all our friends into mannequins? How?"

"I don't know," I said. "All I know is that they're after us. We've got to get away while we still can."

"I'm so scared," whimpered Lisa. "We'll never get away."

"We can't give up now," I said. "Come on. Try to get up. We have to get out into the main part of the mall and find the exit. And we'll stay in crowds. Maybe they won't come after us if they can't get us alone."

I tried not to look down as we tiptoed toward the door. Mannequins were strewn across the floor like corpses.

The girl in the French braid had left in a hurry and had forgotten to lock the door. I opened it a crack and looked out into the brightly lighted hall with closed office doors on both sides.

"The employee entrance!" I cried. "If we can find it, we can get out without going through the part of the mall where the stores are."

Lisa nodded. "But which way is it?"

I looked up and down the hallway. Both directions looked the same. I couldn't remember which side the door had been on when we ducked into it. It had been only a few hours ago, but it seemed more like a year.

"Come on," I said. "We'll have to take a chance."

I took off down the hall. Lisa was right behind me.

"Why don't we try to find an empty office to hide in?" she called to me.

"That wouldn't solve anything," I called back over my shoulder. "We'd still be in the mall with them, and we couldn't stay in there forever. We'd have to come out sometime."

Rounding a corner, I saw a large door at the end of the hall.

We're out of here! I thought ecstatically. It was either the employees' door or the entrance to the mall floor. Either one was better than where we were now.

When I pushed open the door, my heart sank.

"Oh, no," cried Lisa. "We're back in the mall."

I blinked at the sight of the escalators moving slowly up and down, the waterfall tumbling into the goldfish pond, the laughing, talking shoppers lugging bags and packages. They were totally unaware of what was happening right under their noses. They had no idea that innocent kids were being turned into lifeless mannequins all around them.

We darted through the crowd, running without looking back until a pain in my side made me stop and lean against a jewelry-store window.

I bent over, holding my side, and let my chest heave until the pain stopped and I could catch my breath.

"We made it this far," I finally managed to say. "We're going to get away."

"Let's look for a pay phone. I'll call my dad to come after us," offered Lisa.

I shook my head. "We don't have that much

time. The buses run every fifteen minutes. Come on, let's hurry."

As I pushed myself away from the jewelry-store window, I could see someone coming out of the store. It was the girl with the black French braid!

"Come on in, girls. Wouldn't you like to try on some pretty earrings?" she asked sweetly.

"Lisa, don't look in her eyes," I warned as we hurried on past.

Two doors down the blonde in the miniskirt rushed out of a bookstore and shouted, "Come on in, girls. Everything's on sale today."

"Keep going," I ordered Lisa. "Faster."

As we passed an open-air T-shirt shop in the center of the mall, the boy from the video store blocked our way.

"Hey, I've got some great deals on some far-out T's! Come in and look!"

"No! No! We don't want any T-shirts!" I shouted.

"No T-shirts? How about playing a super new video game?" he said, laughing crazily. "Or maybe you'd like to go to a movie. They're all first-run hits." His eyes were wild, and he was lunging toward us.

"No! Leave us alone," I said, pushing him away and running.

"Let go!" I heard Lisa scream.

I looked back. The boy had grabbed Lisa. I saw her struggle wildly and break loose from his grip.

Lisa was crying as she ran toward me.

As we raced past the goldfish pond, she grabbed my arm and stopped.

"What's the matter?" I demanded. "Come on. Let's get out of here!"

Her face was ashen. "Oh, my gosh! Eric! I saw him go into a sporting-goods store called Extra Innings when you went into the video arcade and Shannon and I split up to shop. What if he's still in there?"

"Oh, no," I breathed. "We've got to find him and get him out of here, too. Do you remember where the store is?"

"I think so. It's . . . No, it's . . ." Lisa turned first one direction and then another. "There it is," she said, pointing up to the next level. "See the sign? It says Extra Innings."

I ran for the escalator, praying that Eric would be there and that he was all right. The ride up to the second level seemed to take forever. I could swear the escalator slowed to half speed as soon as we stepped on. When I got off at the top, I turned to tell Lisa to hurry.

I couldn't believe it. She wasn't there!

"Lisa!" I shrieked, jumping up and down to see better. "Lisa, where are you?"

An older couple who were stepping off glared at me.

I looked down the escalator as it continued its

slow rise to the second floor, where person after person got off and went on their way.

But Lisa wasn't with them. She wasn't among the crowd on the first floor waiting to get on the escalator, either.

She was gone.

Lisa had vanished. I was all alone.

Chapter

24

f they had gotten Lisa, they could get me, too. One of them could be standing near me right now. Waiting for me to look around. And when our eyes locked—

"No! No!" I cried.

I ran blindly through the throngs of shoppers. I had to get to Extra Innings and find Eric!

"Excuse me. Excuse me," I muttered over and over as I practically trampled people in my path. Some of them moved out of the way when they heard me coming, but others got angry.

"What a rude girl," I heard someone say.

"That's the younger generation for you," someone else said smugly.

If only they knew, I thought.

I stopped once beside a bridal shop to get my bearings. Without thinking, I glanced up at the bride in the window. Suddenly my eyes widened in alarm. Had she nodded and smiled at me! Was every mannequin in the entire mall under their power?

I tore off through the crowd again as fast as I could go, tripping over a baby stroller and almost falling on my face.

"Excuse me," I said to the mother, stopping only long enough to make sure the baby was all right.

I had to get help, but first I had to find Eric. I could see the sign for Extra Innings just ahead.

Fear was smothering me. I tried not to look at the mannequins in the store windows I was passing, but I knew they were moving. Smiling. Nodding. Reaching toward me. Their eyes followed me. Did that one raise her hand? Did another one blink?

I had to find Eric and drag him to the bus stop. We would get out of there as fast as we could, and on the bus I would tell him about Shannon and Lisa and all the others who had been discarded in the mannequin storeroom. He would believe me this time! And then later—a lot later—we would go back to the mall together, and we would figure out what to do.

Inside the front door to Extra Innings was the ski-equipment department. Eric won't be here, I thought as I hurried through. He loved to play tennis. I would probably find him in the tennis department.

I stood on tiptoes, trying to see which direction to go, but I couldn't spot any sign of the tennis things. I inched past the workout equipment, every nerve in my body alert.

"Eric," I called out, but my voice was small and thin. "Eric! Where are you?"

"Can I help you, miss?"

I froze. The voice was familiar. *Too* familiar. I was face-to-face with the same teenage boy who had been in Cinema Six. And in the video arcade. And the T-shirt shop.

He was smiling. But above his smile, his eyes glinted cold and hard.

I looked away quickly, but he stopped me with a hand.

"Can I help you, miss?" he repeated.

I swallowed hard. I couldn't wait around to find Eric. I had to get out of there!

I could hear my own ragged breathing as I began slowly to back away from the boy. I didn't dare look into his eyes. But I didn't dare turn my back on him either.

Suddenly I bumped against something. I turned my head slightly, catching sight of a tennis racket out of the corner of my eye. I let out a scream.

The racket was in a mannequin's hand.

And that mannequin looked exactly like Eric!

Chapter

I don't remember leaving Extra Innings. I don't remember racing through the mall. I don't even remember entering the bus-stop shelter and curling up in a ball in the corner. But when I finally got the nerve to open my eyes, that's where I was. And it was dark outside!

I glanced at my watch. It was almost time for Wonderland Mall to close for the night, and I was alone at the bus stop. In the silence I could hear the pounding of my heart. Nothing else.

I jumped up and raced to the window, looking toward the highway.

"Come on, bus," I whispered. "Get here. I have to get away. Oh, bus, please. Come on!"

I don't know how long I stood there, watching for the bus to approach, afraid that at any moment one of the freaks from the mall would come after me.

Finally I turned away from the window. I looked at my watch again and then at the schedule on the wall. The last bus should have been here five minutes ago. In twenty minutes the mall doors would be locked. If no more buses came, I would be stuck out here at the bus stop. Alone.

I couldn't take that chance. But what else could I do? I couldn't start out on foot. It was a long way into town, and the highway was dark and lonely. And there was no place else to hide. There was only one possibility left. I had to go back inside before the mall closed and find a phone. I would call home and ask Mom to pick me up.

"Then everything will be okay, and I'll be safe," I said out loud, trying to reassure myself.

My legs were almost too weak to hold me up as I went back inside. I looked around fearfully, but the three evil teenagers were not in sight. Then I hurriedly checked the directory. A bank of telephones was near the escalators.

I could hear the sound of my own footsteps echoing off the walls as I raced toward the phones. Few shoppers remained now, and in the silence the tiny waterfall by the fish pond in the gigantic center court sounded like Niagara Falls.

When I reached the bank of four phones, I couldn't believe my eyes. They were all occupied. Yet there were scarcely four more people still walking around in the mall.

Hurry up! I wanted to scream.

I paced back and forth for a couple of minutes, but no one hung up. Then I remembered that I had seen a second bank of phones on the map. They were at the far end of the mall.

I looked at my watch again. Ten minutes till closing time. I looked around frantically. Still no sign of the three teenagers.

This time my shoes clattered loudly on the concrete floor as I ran toward the phones, but I didn't care. I had to call home—and fast.

This phone bank was empty. I dug change out of my belt bag and shoved it into the slot on the pay phone. My fingers shook as I punched in the number and listened to ring number one. Two. Three.

"Come on, somebody!" I muttered under my breath. "Answer!"

Four. Five. What was I going to do if my parents had gone out? Who else could I call?

Glancing around in desperation, I stopped cold. The telephone receiver slipped slowly out of my hand and clunked against the wall. I could hear a tiny voice saying hello, but I was too horrified to move.

Directly across the hall from the bank of phones was the jewelry store Lisa and I had passed just before she disappeared. In the display case a mannequin head was wearing a glittering diamond tiara, a sparkling necklace of rubies and emeralds, and matching earrings.

The head had thick curly hair and a big smile.

I backed up to the wall in horror, sliding slowly down to the floor. "Lisa?" I whimpered.

I sat there staring at the head. Of all my friends that had come to the mall together, I was the only one left.

Just then I heard the mall's doors slam shut and the automatic locks clang into place.

Chapter

26

I rose slowly to my feet.

The corridors were deserted now. The skylights dark. Silence was everywhere. The mall was closed for the night.

But I was still in it. And I was alone. Alone with three deranged teenagers.

My throat tightened as I tiptoed along.

The main mall lights had been turned off, but inside each of the stores the mannequins in the windows stood out in eerie relief against soft security lights. Their arms were extended toward me as if they were motioning for me to join them.

Beyond the stores—what seemed like at least a thousand miles away—was the mall entrance. I took a deep breath and tried to run for it. Blood thundered in my temples, and all the nerves in my body were poised like porcupine quills.

Suddenly I spotted someone coming toward me from the opposite end of the mall. My heart jumped.

"Oh, please! Let it be a store employee! Or a security guard!"

I blinked and squinted through the shadowy light.

I raised my hand and started to yell.

My hand stopped in midair.

Walking toward me was the beautiful blond teenager in the miniskirt. She was hurrying straight at me!

I spun around and tried to run in the other direction. I needed to find another door!

Coming from that end of the mall was the salesboy. A cry escaped from my throat as I turned again. Looking up, I saw the girl with the black French braid riding down the escalator.

Slowly I became aware of a sound—a soft rustling that grew until I realized that it wasn't a rustling at all. It was voices. Whispers.

"Fa-gin. Fa-gin. Fa-gin."

The whispers sounded unbelievably familiar. I knew where I had heard them before. In the mall basement early that morning. It was when all my friends had already gone, and I was alone beside the crack that had mysteriously opened in the floor and had been cemented up again. I had thought it was the air-conditioning machines.

"FA-GIN! FA-GIN! FA-GIN!"

As the angry whispers swirled around me, I forced my legs to run. But as I ran, so did the mannequins. They started leaving their pedestals in the store windows and moving stiffly after me, like the monster in an old Frankenstein movie.

"FA-GIN! FA-GIN! FA-GIN!"

I lunged toward the double glass doors, praying that someone would be out there and I could call for help. Outside, only a lone car sat under a light post. It was empty. I could see the highway beyond. I could see *freedom!* If only I could get there.

My legs were pumping, my lungs screaming for air as I put every last ounce of energy I had into getting away.

I reached out, almost touching the door, when I skidded to a halt. The beautiful blonde, the salesboy, and the girl with the dark French braid had somehow blocked my way.

Every muscle in my body shuddered with exhaustion.

There was no escape. Nowhere to run.

I was trapped.

I turned slowly around to face the parade of mannequins coming in my direction. They had lost their stiffness now, and they danced toward me with outstretched arms.

To my horror, leading the parade was a man-

111

nequin with white-blonde hair, one with wire-rimmed glasses, a boy mannequin carrying a tennis racket, and a laughing jewelry-store head, floating and bobbing in the air.

Chapter

27

The blonde in the miniskirt snapped her fingers. The ghostly parade stopped on command. The whispers stopped too. It was deadly silent as the mannequins shuffled forward to form a circle around me.

I looked from one of my friends to another. The painted smiles remained on each of their faces, but above the smiles, their eyes had grown sorrowful. As I stared at Jamie, a tear rolled down her shiny plastic cheek.

"What do you *want*?" I screamed, turning to the three teenagers who had joined me inside the circle.

"Revenge," whispered the blonde.

"Wheels," said the boy.

"Life," said the girl with the French braid.

"I don't understand!" I cried. "Why are you doing this?"

The boy sneered. "We were too young to die when we got lost in Mournful Swamp."

"Our friends all grew up, but we didn't," said the blonde. Her voice sounded like a moan.

"It wasn't fair," snapped the girl with the French braid. "We want what we missed out on."

The blonde nodded somberly. "And all we got was a cold, lonely grave at the bottom of the Mournful Swamp ravine."

I blinked at them in astonishment. "I . . . I know who you are," I whispered. "You're the teenagers who disappeared in Mournful Swamp a long time ago."

"That's right," said the girl with the French braid. "The mall construction disturbed our grave and made us restless. We want to live again. To *party*." She looked at the boy and grinned.

"Yeah," he said, grinning back at her. "To get some wheels and cruise."

"And when the crack in the mall floor appeared right over our graves, we knew the perfect chance had come," said the blonde. "It was like a door opening up for us so that we could escape back into life again—the life we had missed."

"But to do it we had to trade our existence for yours," said the boy.

"Now it's your turn to spend eternity watching your friends laughing and having fun, while you stand silently by and watch," said the girl with the

French braid. She snickered. "After all, don't all teenagers come to the mall? You'll see everyone you know."

My heart was in my throat. "Do you mean that you're stealing back your lives by turning innocent kids into mannequins?" I asked incredulously. I looked back at the sea of plastic faces with their mournful eyes. "Into lifeless zombies?"

The blonde nodded and moved toward me. Her eyes were glowing with an unearthly brilliance. Her voice was low and menacing.

"And you're next, Robin Fagin."

Chapter

28

I tried to back away, but she kept advancing toward me. The other two ghosts were coming at me from each side.

I could feel their eyes burning into my face, but I didn't dare look at them. I knew what their eyes could do to me. Hypnotize me. Put me in a trance so that I would be in their power. And then, when I was helpless, they would draw the life out of me, leaving only a shell.

A mannequin.

Just like my friends.

Behind the ghosts, the mannequins stirred restlessly. Their arms moved stiffly up and down, and the smiling jewelry-store head nodded, as if agreeing that I was about to join her fate.

Then the whispers started again.

"Fa-gin. Fa-gin. Fa-gin."

I clamped my hands over my ears to shut out the awful sound.

I was alone! There was no escape! No one to save me!

"FA-GIN. FA-GIN. FA-GIN."

The whispers had turned to shouts. The ghosts were nearer. Grinning.

The mannequins closed around me. Suffocating me.

"FA-GIN! FA-GIN! FA-GIN!"

I took a deep breath. I had to do something to save myself. There was only one chance.

"Stop it! I can help you!" I screamed.

Everything stopped. The ghosts stood facing me like stone statues. The mannequins were silent and motionless, as if someone had thrown a switch, shutting them down.

"How?" challenged the blonde. "How can *you* help *us*?"

I took a deep breath to slow the pounding of my heart. "Wheels!" I said. My voice boomed in the silent mall and echoed faintly off the skylights.

"Wheels?" the boy asked excitedly. "What do you mean, wheels?"

"I know where there's a car," I said. "You could cruise. Party. Really live again the way you want to."

"Where?" The boy looked eagerly around.

I hesitated. I couldn't tell them about the one

car left in the parking lot. They might go after it themselves and leave me here, after they transformed me into a plastic dummy. But if I could persuade them to open the door and follow me, maybe I could get away from them. Run for my life!

"I'll have to show you," I said in a faltering voice.

The ghost with the black French braid bounced up and down with excitement. "Oh, let's do it!"

"It would be like before," the blonde said breathlessly. "Like when we were *alive*."

"That's right," I said, trying to keep my voice steady. "You don't want to stay in this stupid mall, do you? Not when you could cruise all night long. Anywhere you wanted to cruise. For as long as you wanted to."

A faraway smile appeared on the boy's face, and his eyes danced, as if he were imagining it all.

I held my breath and listened to the pounding of my heart. He had to say yes. It was my only chance to escape. My only chance to stay alive!

"Okay," he said. "Let's go."

He shoved past me and pushed open the double doors. The security alarm blasted in our ears. He ignored it, stalking out into the night. I was right behind him. I could hear the other two ghosts following.

"There it is," I shouted, pointing to the car sitting

119

under the lamppost. "Go get it. It's all yours."

At the sight of the car, the boy broke into a run. He seemed to have forgotten all about me. Now was my chance!

I veered off toward the main highway and hurled myself into the darkness.

Maybe I could flag down a car. Hitch a ride into town. Get help.

Just then I heard the girls shouting.

"Look! She's getting away!"

"After her!"

I didn't dare look back. My legs were pumping like pistons. My lungs gasping for air.

The highway was still far away, and they were gaining on me. I could hear their feet pounding on the asphalt.

I ran on, praying I could make it.

Then I caught a faint sound on the night wind. A low moan that built into a wail.

"Ooooohhh! Aaaaawww!"

I glanced over my shoulder and gasped in horror. Three pairs of ancient gnarled hands reached out for me. Three wrinkled toothless faces gaped at me.

"Robin! Robin!" screamed the old hag in the miniskirt. Her once beautiful blond hair hung in long white tatters.

Skin was falling away from the face of the boy ghost, revealing ghastly patches of white skull. The fingers that reached toward me weren't fingers anymore. They were turning into bones.

The ghost with the French braid let out a blood-curdling scream and clutched her face as an eye-ball popped out of its socket and rolled across the ground.

They had grown hideously old in the few seconds since they had left the mall, and they were disintegrating—all three of them—rotting right before my eyes.

But they still managed to stumble after me with amazing speed, screaming my name over and over.

Suddenly I tripped. My legs flew out from under me, sending me sprawling onto the ground. I struggled to get up. I could hear their pounding feet behind me! Coming closer!

They were there! I could see three ghoulish faces over me. Bony fingers forcing my face to turn toward theirs. Livid eyes staring into mine. The stench of the swamp gagged me as their hot breath wrapped around me like a blanket of decay.

I felt myself slipping away. Floating out of consciousness and into a world of darkness. I had failed. I was theirs.

Forever.

Chapter

Suddenly the air around me seemed to change and grow cooler. The smell of decay drifted slowly away.

I opened my eyes. A million stars twinkled above me. I wasn't in the land of blackness I had been heading toward a moment ago. I was still in the parking lot of Wonderland Mall.

Then something caught my eye. Movement. My heart jumped into my throat.

I raised my head and stared in amazement at three shadows, whirling at an incredible speed. They were hurrying away from me and toward the mall.

"Oh, my gosh!" I whispered aloud. "It's them! The ghosts!"

Suddenly I understood. They had strayed too far from their grave and from the life force they had stolen from my friends. Now they were trying to save themselves by getting back inside the mall!

I stumbled to my feet, holding my breath as they sped toward the same double glass doors we had come out of only moments before.

No! I screamed silently. *You can't make it back inside! You must be destroyed!*

As I watched, the figures began to change again. Withering like autumn leaves in a flame and falling to the ground into three small piles of ashes outside the doors.

Tears of relief and joy rolled down my face. They were gone, and I was alive!

I looked up at the sound of faint moaning. *Was it the wind?* I wondered, and shivered. *Or the last angry cries of the ghosts?*

An instant later a breeze picked up the ashes and swirled them one more time, whisking them past me in little dust devils and away into the night. As they blew by my face, I caught the distinct stench of the swamp.

Suddenly the mall doors burst open, and dozens of boys and girls raced out into the parking lot.

"Robin! Robin!"

Jamie was running toward me with her arms flung open wide. "I got to the mall late, and I couldn't find you! Where have you been?"

"It's a long story," I said, laughing and hugging her tightly. Shannon, Lisa, and Eric were gathering around me, too. And I saw Aaron Stemple and the girl from my social-studies class in the crowd. And Kitty López and Diane Davies. Everyone was giggling and talking at once.

Shannon pushed her glasses up on her nose and looked around, frowning. "Hey, guys, it's night. I didn't realize we had been in the mall that long."

"Me, either," said Lisa. "My mom will kill me if I don't get home."

"And look," said Kitty. "The mall's *closed*."

I shook my head in amazement. They didn't remember being mannequins! They didn't remember anything that had happened to them!

The sound of a siren was building in the distance, and a moment later a police car with flashing lights turned into the mall's parking lot. I had forgotten all about setting off the security alarm.

There's going to be a lot of explaining to do, I thought with a sigh. But I certainly could never tell anyone the truth. Nobody would ever believe that something like this could happen, *not in a million years*.

Then I glanced at Eric. He looked back and smiled.

His dimple appeared like magic.

Here's a Sneak Preview of Bone Chillers #2: Little Pet Shop of Horrors. . . .

Cassidy Cavanaugh brought her bike to a skidding stop. She stared at the small red brick building. "Look at that pet shop," she said, pointing. "I don't remember seeing it before. Where'd it come from?"

She and her best friend, Suki Chen, were out riding their bikes. It was a scorching hot summer afternoon, and they were trying to cool off.

"Me either," said Suki. "It's weird. There was an empty lot there the last time we came by."

"Yeah, that's what I thought," agreed Cassie. "But they couldn't have built a whole building in one week. And look at the vines. They're growing all the way up to the roof. Even mutant vines don't grow that fast."

Suki shrugged and flipped her straight black hair over one shoulder. "Who cares? I'm roasting out

127

here. Let's go back to my house and blast the air-conditioning."

Cassie shook her head and stared at the building. It looked old—really old. She wondered if maybe they'd built it with antique bricks to make it look that way.

"You just want to go home so you can practice gymnastics," she said to Suki. "I want to go check out the store. I bet they have some cute puppies in there."

It annoyed Cassie that gymnastics was practically the only thing Suki cared about. Especially since Cassie couldn't even do a decent cartwheel. Cassie was too big to be a gymnast anyway.

All the gymnasts Cassie had ever seen were small and cute, like Suki. None of them were tall and bony like Cassie. *I need binoculars to see past my knobby knees all the way to my feet—my huge feet*, she thought.

"You know I've got to practice for that meet next Saturday," complained Suki. "It's a really big deal."

"And you know how much I love animals," said Cassie. "I want to see what they've got in that store. It'll only take a couple of minutes."

"Oh, all right," Suki said. "But I'm out of there if they have any snakes. I *hate* snakes!"

They walked their bikes to the front of the store.

It wasn't much like any pet store Cassie had seen.

Usually pet stores had big windows, so that you could look inside and see all the cute, cuddly puppies and kittens. This one just had a bulletin board inside one small window. It had pictures of dogs and cats thumbtacked to it. It reminded her of the "WANTED" posters for criminals they had in the post office.

Cassie read a sign, which was posted over the bulletin board:

CUSTOM PETS
TELL US EXACTLY WHAT TYPE PET YOU'RE
LOOKING FOR, AND WE'LL FIND IT FOR YOU.
SATISFACTION GUARANTEED!!!

Suki opened the door, and Cassie followed her inside.

The walls of the store were lined with cages, but most of them were empty. A single light bulb was hanging from the center of the ceiling. It cast a dim glow over everything, making it hard to see. Cassie walked over to check out the animals in the cages.

"This is a pretty lame pet shop," said Suki. "They really don't have much."

Only three of the cages had dogs in them. Another held two kittens.

When they saw the girls, the dogs started frantically pawing at the doors to their cages. The kittens started meowing and walking in circles.

Cassie knelt down in front of a cage with a

Siberian Husky puppy inside. Its fur was soft and fluffy. "Ohhh, poor thing. He's lonely."

The husky pushed up against the door and looked up at Cassie. She stuck her fingers through the bars and scratched it on its neck.

The puppy whimpered.

"He's got the saddest eyes," Cassie cooed. "I'd love to take him home with me."

Cassie suddenly felt a tickle in the back of her nose.

"AH-AH-AH-CHOO!" Cassie sneezed. "Darn it! AH-CHOO!" she sneezed again.

"Bless you," Suki said. "With your allergies, Cassie . . . that puppy would probably make you sneeze yourself to death."

"Bless you!" said a voice.

Cassie rubbed her nose and turned to see who had said that.

Sitting behind the counter, on a stool, was a very pale and incredibly fat man. He looked like a giant bullfrog propped on a lily pad.

Cassie squinted in the dim light, trying to see the man's face.

His eyes were bulging out of their sockets. His mouth was wide and thin. He didn't seem to have lips. He was gross!

"Thanks," she murmured, trying to throw off the creepy feeling he gave her.

"My name is Mr. Willard. Can I help you young

ladies?" he wheezed from his perch on the stool.

"No, we're just looking," said Suki. "Come on, Cassie. You promised we'd just stay a minute."

"I'm sure I can show you a pet that would interest you," said Mr. Willard. Struggling to get down off his stool, he waddled toward them. "If one of these animals isn't satisfactory, I can get you any kind of pet you want," he said. "Any kind at all."

Cassie could smell his sour breath. And she couldn't help noticing his eyes. They were solid black and watery, like a giant bug's.

Cassie heard a whine behind her and looked back at the puppy. Was it begging to come with her?

"Come on, Cassie. You promised," said Suki tugging at her arm.

"Okay," Cassie answered reluctantly.

She looked over her shoulder as they left the shop. The clerk was staring at her with his black watery eyes.

"You'll be back," he said.

Then he laughed.

On the way to Suki's house, they passed by City Park. *I'd really rather ride my bike in the park than stay inside at Suki's. Who cares about the stupid old air-conditioning*, thought Cassie. When you pedal fast, the breeze keeps you plenty cool.

"Hey, David, come on! Let *me* play with it. Pleeeze!"

Cassie heard a boy's voice nearby. It sounded like some boys from her school. She and Suki stopped their bikes to see what was going on.

"As usual, David Ferrante's showing off for this friends," said Suki.

Cassie shaded her eyes from the bright sunlight. She could see David and four other boys from their class huddled in a circle. David was holding a small white box. Cassie noticed that the box had holes in its sides.

David opened the top just long enough for the others to peek inside. Then he slammed it shut.

"Come on, David. I didn't even get to see it," cried Max Neal.

"Me either," complained Todd Cook. "Keep the lid off longer."

"Too bad. It's my turn next," said Ken Coffey, elbowing his way closer to David.

"I wonder what he's got in that box," said Cassie.

"Who cares?" said Suki, heaving a bored sigh. "Maybe it's his brains. They're certainly tiny enough to fit in that box. Let's go. I can hear the air-conditioning calling me, can't you?"

"Get serious," said Cassie. "I've got to know what's in that box. Do you think David would let us see it?"

"Ca-*aassi!*" moaned Suki. "Have you totally lost it? You know the kind of stupid jokes David Ferrante is always pulling. It's probably something disgusting."

"I know, but . . ." said Cassie. She put her foot on the pedal to leave. Then she stopped. It really bugged her when people kept secrets from her.

David raised the lid a couple of inches, holding the box up so that Ken Coffey could peak in. The next instant he slammed the lid shut again.

"Aaaahiiieee!" Ken cried. "Totally cool! Let me see it again! Come on, David! Let me *see* it!"

"Now, I've *got* to find out what's in that box," Cassie said.

She pushed down the kickstand, angled the front wheel so that the bike would stand up on its own, and marched toward the group of boys.

They were so intent on the box that none of them noticed her.

"David, can I *see?*" she asked sweetly.

David looked up and grinned. "It's Hopalong Cassidy!" he teased. "Hey, everybody, say hi to Hopalong!"

Cassie's face turned bright red with embarrassment as the boys broke into wild laughter.

Shouts of "Hi, Hopalong!" filled the air.

Cassie *hated* it when David called her Hopalong. David knew that, so he did it all the time. It was even worse when he got other kids to say it, too.

133

"David Ferrante, you are such a jerk!" she yelled, spinning around and heading back for her bike.

"Hey, Hopalong, where are you going?" he called. "I thought you wanted to see what's in the box."

Cassie stopped. She knew that it was dangerous to trust David. But it was all she could do to keep from turning around.

"Come here," David coaxed. "I'll let you see if you want to. Don't you want to see?"

"Ignore him, Cassie," Suki warned. She had parked her bike and was heading toward them.

"Come on, Suki-Pukey. You can see, too," David said.

"Listen, you jerk!" Cassie cried, angrily advancing on David. "You—"

Suddenly David held the box out toward her and took the lid off. It was almost under her nose. She couldn't help but look inside.

"*Eeeeyuk!*" Cassie squealed.

A giant tarantula was staring back at her with beady black eyes! Its long hairy front legs waved as if it were reaching out for her.

The tarantula was lunging right at Cassie's face.

About the Author

Betsy Haynes has written over fifty books for children, including *The Great Mom Swap,* the bestselling The Fabulous Five series, and the Taffy Sinclair books. *Taffy Goes to Hollywood* received the Phantom's Choice Award for Best Juvenile Series Book of 1990.

When she isn't writing, Betsy loves to travel, and she and her husband, Jim, spend as much time as possible aboard their boat, *Nut & Honey.* Betsy and her husband live on Marco Island, Florida, and have two grown children, two dogs, and a black cat with extra toes.

▰ HarperPaperbacks *By Mail*

This collection of spine-tingling horrors will scare you silly! Be sure
not to miss any of these eerie tales.

BONE CHILLERS

#1 Beware the Shopping Mall
Robin's heard weird things about Wonderland Mall. She's heard it's haunted.
When she and her friends go shopping there, she knows something creepy is
watching. Something that's been dead for a long, long time.

#2 Little Pet Shop of Horrors
Cassie will do anything for a puppy. She'll even spend the night alone in a
spooky old pet shop. But Cassie doesn't know that the shop's weird owner has
a surprise for her. She can play with the puppies as long as she wants. She can
stay in the pet shop . . . forever!

#3 Back to School
Fitzgerald Traflon III hates the food at Maple Grove Middle School—it's totally
gross. Then Miss Buggy takes over the cafeteria, and things start to change. Fitz's
friends love Miss Buggy's cooking, but Fitz still won't eat it. Soon his friends are
acting really strange. And the more they eat . . . the weirder they get!

#4 Frankenturkey
Kyle and Annie want to celebrate Thanksgiving like the Pilgrims. They even want
to raise their own turkey. Then they meet Frankenturkey! Frankenturkey is big.
Frankenturkey is bad. If Kyle and Annie don't watch out, Frankenturkey will eat
them for Thanksgiving dinner.

- -

MAIL TO: Harper Collins Publishers
P.O.Box 588, Dunmore, PA 18512-0588

TELEPHONE: 1-800-331-3761 (Visa and Mastercard holders!)

YES, please send me the following titles:

Bone Chillers
❏ #1 Beware the Shopping Mall (0-06-106176-X) $3.50
❏ #2 Little Pet Shop of Horrors (0-06-106206-5)....................................$3.50
❏ #3 Back to School (0-06-106186-7) $3.50
❏ #4 Frankenturkey (0-06-106197-2)...$3.50

SUBTOTAL...$_____
POSTAGE AND HANDLING* ....$____2.00____
SALES TAX (Add applicable state sales tax) ....$_____

TOTAL: ....$_____
(Remit in U.S. funds. Do not send cash.)

NAME _____

ADDRESS _____

CITY _____

STATE _____ ZIP _____

Allow up to six weeks for delivery. Prices subject to change. Valid only in U.S. and Canada.

*Free postage/handling if you buy four or more!